A

W.A.S.

(Withstand All Strife to Heal)

"Maisha's book is so timely for the culture. It is my belief that her story will help all women, but specifically Black women move away from the cultural belief that only weak women have mental health challenges. Through her vulnerability, Maisha powerfully depicts how someone like herself, perceived as strong and accomplished, privately battled for her life to ultimately reclaim it.

W.A.S.H. will shift the narrative about what it means to be strong in the presence of life's challenges and provide a pathway for other women to share their struggles and receive healing through the process of self-reflection and doing their dirty laundry." If you haven't listened to Kelly Rowland's song entitled "Dirty Laundry" ...please do so. Maisha has written her own declaration for doing the work necessary to heal.

~Latika Davis-Jones, PhD.

W.A.S.H.: *Time To Do YOUR Laundry*

Published by InTouch Consulting

InTouch
consulting

Cover Design: Soleil Meade, Soleil Branding Essentials
Internal Book Layout: InSCRIBEd Inspiration, LLC.

Printed in the United States of America

ISBN: 978-1692797560

W.A.S.H.:

Time To Do YOUR Laundry

W.A.S.H.:

Time To Do YOUR Laundry

Maisha Howze, MS.

InTouch
consulting

ACKNOWLEDGEMENTS

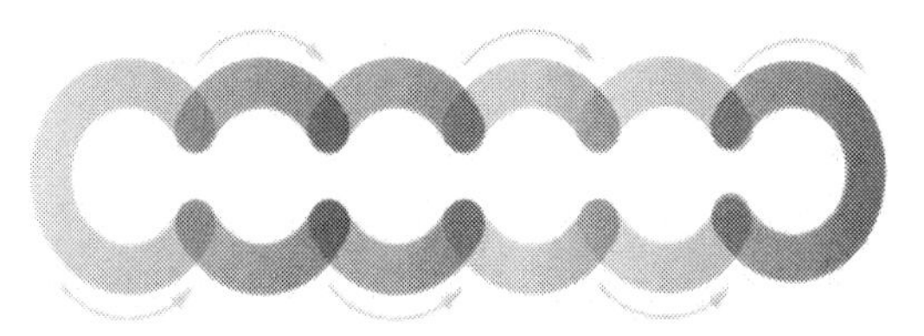

Words truly cannot express how grateful I am to have received so much support on this journey to complete **W.A.S.H.**, *Time To Do YOUR Laundry*. Everyone supported my process without hesitation.

When I contacted Nicole Narvaez in March of 2019 to ask if she would have time to mentor me through the process to complete my book, her exact words were, "For you? Of course!" Nicole coached me through the process and remained committed. I am truly grateful for her support.

Rosa Davis, the Foreword truly captured the essence of **W.A.S.H.**

Thank you to first readers: Amy Wienand, Amy Sula, Leslie Slagel, Erica Hines-McGee, Kecia Marshall, Denele Biggs, Teliah McCaskill, Felicia Robinson, Mrs. Elnora Biggs and Danetria Craig. They offered honest and thoughtful feedback which helped to ensure I was speaking from a universal perspective.

Thank you, Dr. Latika Davis Jones, for your advanced praise of **W.A.S.H.**

I am grateful for the spiritual covering of Amy Boyd and Angelique Strothers through the process of **W.A.S.H.**

TABLE OF CONTENTS
W.A.S.H.: *Time To Do YOUR Laundry*

Foreword i

Preface iii

PART I 1

The Stains in My Life 1

Real Feelings 2

Childhood Stains 8
Something Changed 13

Young Adult Stains 16
Not Again 20

PART II 25

Internal Cleansing 25
Correlation 28

Chapter 1 33

The Dirty Clothes Hamper 33

I Do Not Like What I See 35

You Matter 36

Chapter 2 41

Sorting 41

Internal Sorting 42

Preserving Integrity 45

Generational Issues 47
What is the Depth of the Stain? 48
Harmful 50
Prioritizing 51
Chapter 3 55
Preparation 55
Choosing Your Cleaning Agent/Detergent 56
Load The Washer 57
Select Water Temperature 58
Difference in Water Temperatures 58
Select the Cycle 59
The Normal Cycle 60
The Permanent Press Cycle 60
The Delicate Cycle 61
Add Cleaning Agent/ Detergent 62
Pre-Soak 63
Chapter 4 69
Hit Start 69
What Do You Need to Hit Start? 70
What Is Your Mental and Emotional State? 71
What Is Your Spiritual State? 72
What Is the State of Your Self-Awareness? 73
What Are Your Identified Issues Being Addressed? 74
Chapter 5 79
The Agitation 79
The Uncomfortable Feeling of Being Agitated 86
Chapter 6 91
Rinse Cycle 91
What About You? 94
Are You Ready for Your Downpour? 94

Chapter 7 97

The Spin Cycle 97

PART III 101

Finishing Touches 101
    Line Dry 102
    Tumble Dry, Normal 102
    Dots 102
    Dashes 102

Folding, Hanging and Putting Away 105

Final Thoughts 107

About the Author 109

References 111

FOREWORD

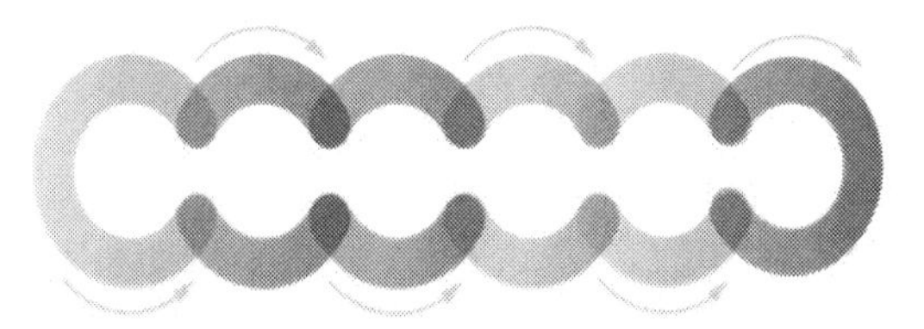

Margaret Thatcher said, "You may have to fight a battle more than once to win it." Maisha Howze very cleverly reminds us of this while inspiring hope . . . hope that we absolutely have the power to 'win' when we face whatever has been holding us back from experiencing joy.

Maisha's **W.A.S.H.**, takes the reader through a process of washing away pain and suffering; healing from traumas experienced once or throughout a lifetime. She does it by comparing the process to that of washing clothes. From the decision to "do laundry" to sorting the clothes to selecting the right temperature and wash cycle to the uncomfortable, but necessary, phase of agitation – Maisha describes the progression of healing.

I met Maisha early in her career when she was a Resource Coordinator at our residential treatment program more than 20 years ago. She was smart, dedicated, resilient, hard-working, and genuinely interested in the lives of the women we served. It's absolutely no surprise to me that she has gone on, and continues, to hold leadership positions in her professional life and in her community. Her commitment to and passion for helping people find wholeness has always been apparent. What did come as a surprise was learning that she carried such heavy burdens.

While reading the introduction and first few chapters of this instructional, self-help book that Maisha has written, I found myself wondering how it was that I worked with her and did not know what she was trying to sort out in her head and in her heart. Maisha allows herself to be transparent and vulnerable, and her insights lead her to make the kinds of witty analogies that are easy to relate to and may prompt insights of your own!

As women, we continuously strive for balance in our lives. And, although at times we know what we need to do, 'hitting that start' button can be a challenge. Like those overwhelming loads of laundry, the work of ridding ourselves of pain, guilt, shame, hurt, and disappointment can stop us in our tracks.
After nearly 30 years of leading an organization established to help women reclaim their lives, I've seen firsthand how the devastation and complexity of the disease of addiction can create a sense of hopelessness.

For those suffering from a substance use problem or for anyone dealing with issues that prevent them from fully appreciating and experiencing their own self-worth, **W.A.S.H.**, offers some simple steps for beginning to explore how to renew and reset. We all need to build our toolkits . . . consider this as one more tool that just may lead to opening the door to freedom, even if we must open that door more than once.

~Rosa Davis, CEO, POWER

Pennsylvania Organization for Women in Early Recovery helping women reclaim their lives from the disease of addiction to alcohol and other drugs, and to reduce the incidence of addiction in future generations

PREFACE

I consider myself, Uniquely Un-unique. Yes, I am an individual, and there are many different aspects that make up Maisha, but I have experienced some of the same things that others have experienced. I know that my experiences are not unique specifically to me. Often people will tell me that I look like I have it all together, and I tell them that they are seeing what God wants them to see. God knows that others are watching for a variety of reasons, but the bottom line is someone else is watching and people who are struggling need to know that they are not alone!

The details may be unique, but the situations are not. Even if this book only helps one person, that is one more person who knows that they are not alone and can survive and grow, even when they do not see a light. My prayer is that as you experience this book you will grow to love yourself and those around you more and more.

I wrote this book, not just to "tell my story," but with hopes that my story and experiences will help someone else. It is hard when you think that your situation is unique, and no one will understand. I have been there before. It is a hard position to be in. You want to share what you are going through. Sometimes you just want to stand in the middle of a crowded space and yell, "I AM NOT OK!" But fear sets in. The fear of what others will think and how you will move on after being vulnerable.

I want you to be ok with being vulnerable and knowing you can heal. Hopefully, you will also understand while reading this book that although issues may reappear you can reach into your toolkit to know how to handle the situations and not be broken by what you are experiencing.

I deliberately have included real life situations in this book, not because I think that my story is so interesting. Believe me it is not. My situation is not unique. I included my own personal stories because I know that at least one other person has had the same experience or may know someone who has. I want people to know they are not alone. I truly believe in community, and the manifestation of community is love and care. I believe that people become stronger when they know that they are not alone, when they know that in the midst of their struggle someone else has had a similar experience and has emerged stronger, more self-assured, and with a more intense sense of self and healthier spiritual connection.

This book is geared to both men and women. Both genders complete the chore of laundry. Although I think men and women may respond to emotional situations differently, I believe both will have to go through the cleansing process at some point in their life.

I want you to examine the similarities between the process of doing laundry and the process of internal cleansing of self. There is a sincere correlation between the two. Why do we complete the chore of laundry? Why do we put our clothes through that intense process? Is there a benefit? We do this to preserve our investment and show appreciation for what belongs to us. Regardless if we purchased the clothing or if it was gifted to us, we understand the basics of not allowing old smells and stains to rest on our valued fabrics.

I began to think more and more about the process and how it correlates with removing the stains of your life. How the cycles correlate to steps that you could take to rid your life of those stains that may have caused damage.

As there are steps to doing laundry there are steps to a person becoming whole (cleansing oneself). Many think the process is as easy as, "I am in a bad "space" or mood so let me use a quick fix to get better or only do some of the work to impact what I am going through. But it is not that easy. Think about when you are doing your laundry; there are steps to follow. If you miss a step there is a chance that your clothing will not become clean, and you will have to repeat the process. Similarly, your internal process requires you to follow a process and completely address your issues (stains) or you will have to repeat the process, and the true healing will be impacted. An even deeper impact of missing steps in the process may leave a stench that lingers. I will address those lingering stenches in your life a little later in the book.

As you read there are a few key terms I want you to keep in mind:

- Defeatist Mindset - constantly expecting the worse
- Helping professionals - People who nurture the growth of, or address the problems of a person's physical, psychological, intellectual, emotional or spiritual well-being
- Integrity - the quality of being honest and having strong moral principles; moral upright
- Laundry Stain - a mark, possibly from dirt that is not easily removed
- Life Stain - those things that have caused damage emotionally, physically, mentally, spiritually, socially, etc.

- Process - A series of actions to achieve a specific goal

PART I
The Stains in My Life

Real Feelings

"Take me now!"

I wanted to kill myself. Suicide was a constant looming thought. There were so many things weighing me down, and I felt like I could not catch a break. I truly did not know how to deal with the pressures of life, and I wanted it all to end.

I awoke one Saturday morning feeling unsettled and unhappy. I was not sure why I was feeling this way, but my life seemed to be very chaotic, and it was as if I did not have a grasp on things in my past, present or future. I was having quick thoughts and flashes of all periods of my life but did not know why they were appearing very rapidly in what seemed to be a consecutive yet random pattern.

"There were so many things weighing me down and I felt like I could not catch a break."

These flashes of my life were creating very scary feelings. I did not understand what was happening, I mean, after all, the sun was shining, my children were healthy, I had a job, food in the refrigerator, family and friends that loved me, and most importantly, a healthy relationship with God and my own personal spiritual connection to Him. I sat on the edge of my bed thinking, "I know things could be a lot worse!" I was having great difficulty understanding this feeling and the mood that I seemed to be developing. I tried to shake it off and start my day. I kept saying to myself, "There is nothing to worry about."

I decided to make breakfast for my children. I washed my face, hands and brushed my teeth. Then I went to the kitchen to get breakfast started, but I was again overwhelmed by this eerie feeling. I was becoming so agitated by what was happening. I immediately thought of another task to do. For some reason I thought one more thing to keep busy would shake this feeling. I decided to put a load of clothes in the wash while I was preparing breakfast.

As I walked down the stairs to the basement, I could see the baskets spilling over with dirty clothes. The internal agitation began to increase. It was so intense, my hands began to tremble, and I broke out in a sweat. I continued down the stairs and stood in the middle of the floor, scanned the room looking at the piles of dirty clothes which to me appeared to cover the entire basement floor and reach as high as the ceiling. The feeling of agitation quickly turned into sadness. Because of the intensity of my sadness, I began to experience anger. I was angry about this unknown feeling. I was angry that in a split second my surroundings seemed so disorderly. I let out a loud frustrated sigh, shook my head, and said, "I'm not dealing with this mess today!" So, I walked back up the stairs, put the breakfast food back in the refrigerator, put out some cereal and milk, walked to my bedroom, got in the bed, curled up into a ball, closed my eyes, and went to sleep.

Take a minute to think about what happened. I was overwhelmed with an intense feeling, and it completely changed the direction of my morning. One moment I was preparing a full breakfast for my children, and in an instant, I decided to feed them processed food. Processed food, the food that has high fructose syrup, preservatives, and other additives with names I cannot pronounce. This is what I decided, to feed my children processed food instead of a cooked breakfast with fresh food. An unhealthy mindset and emotional state can change our direction from a healthy choice to an unhealthy choice. Nonetheless, the laundry remained dirty, and I went into an isolated slumber.

Isolated Slumber is a term I use to describe when you lay down and go to sleep just to avoid surroundings. For some of us, that is our escape from our current reality. The reality of single parenthood, financial struggles, homelessness, addiction, abusive relationships, etc. Although for a moment we can escape, the issues are still present and relevant when we awake.

"Isolated Slumber is a term I use to describe when you lay down and go to sleep just to avoid surroundings."

After a couple hours I awoke feeling tired, irritated and not rested. I realized I slept, but I did not rest. There are times that we sleep but not rest. If you are rested, you will wake refreshed with a renewed strength. You feel like you can handle anything that you face. Have you ever had an important project due and have an uninterrupted night's rest? When you awake, your mind is clear, and you are focused. The opposite happens when you merely sleep but not rest. When you awake, you are still thinking about the concerns from the night before.

I knew that the looming feelings of irritation were still present and my time in bed had not resolved anything. I began to wonder, "What is wrong? What can I do to fix this?" I quickly realized that I had to first figure out what "this" was in order to fix "it". I knew something was wrong and unsettling but could not identify what those things were. I began to evaluate my current situation which eventually forced me to look at my past.

I was a single mom of twins, a boy and a girl, working a full-time job and various contracted positions, and was enrolled as a full-time graduate student. One would say, "Of course your mind is unsettled." But deep down inside, I knew these feelings had nothing to do with all my responsibilities. It was truly about not having peace with some of my past and present situations. I realized I was holding on to resentments, shame, guilt, trauma, anxiety, and depression that would hinder my growth and forward movement.

*"I began to wonder, what is wrong?
What can I do to fix this?*

Childhood Stains

Growing up I struggled with low self-esteem and self-doubt. I was very thin with acne, and I did not have the softest features or light skin (yes, that was a factor). I was teased a lot and internalized all these feelings. I became very defensive and was extremely unhappy. It is natural for one to become "defensive" or guarded when they feel attacked. If one believes they are being attacked, unwarranted or due to something such as their God given appearance, walls may go up.

What I have learned over the years is that although being defensive was my preferred means of protection, I was more than those things that I thought I needed to cover up or change. I realized that I needed to embrace who I am regardless of what others said. I now recognize when I am being defensive, and I try to curve or mute my responses so that my interaction is not perceived as being defensive. This is a work in progress. I have learned that being defensive can significantly impact relationships. Although being defensive is a way to cope and seemingly eliminate the stress you may expect to endure, it can also have a very negative impact on others you are in a relationship with. You begin to create this bleak outlook on every encounter. This can be exhausting for those that you encounter. It can cause you to have a negative relationship with yourself. The bleak outlook can be internalized and affect how you move day to day. It can impact how you think others will engage with you. You may be motivated to prematurely react to situations because of how you

"If one believes they are being attacked, unwarranted or due to something such as their God given appearance, walls may go up."

think you will be perceived or treated. When I was in the sixth grade, I made an extremely premature decision due to how I thought people would treat me.

Who remembers Jheri curls? Well I had one. One day I realized I needed a "touch up" because my roots were consuming the style. I had so much new growth there was an afro under the overly activated strings of hair. I was so afraid of what others would say, I did not want to go to school. So, I decided to straighten my hair. Yup, I decided to put a hot comb to processed hair that had not been washed, conditioned or treated in preparation for a straightening. I had never straightened my own hair and had no idea how hot the comb should be. I grabbed the blue hair grease, a hand towel, and a comb. I turned the fire on high and placed the straightening comb on the burner, parted my hair into sections and greased it while the comb heated up. When I thought it was hot enough, I pulled it from the fire, patted it with the towel because that is what I saw others do and proceeded to straighten my hair. The first stroke of the comb I heard fssssss.

It was difficult to pull the comb through, so I combed out each section, ignoring the continuous fssssss with each stroke. I did not have a mirror, so I was unaware what my hair looked like. I could only feel it, and it felt straighter than before. I finally finished my hair, as I walked to the bathroom the smell of burnt hair grease and CareFree Activation Spray followed me. I looked at my hair and saw that it looked golden. I was in shock. I touched the piece in the front, pulled away my hand, and there was hair in my fingers. Touched another piece, and again, hair in my fingers. I repeated this as there were several gold colored sections.

I did not want my mom to wake up and see me, so I hurried out the door and left for school. I tried to pull it back in a ponytail, but it did not work. I sat on the school bus praying people did not notice, I slouched down as far as I could in my seat. Once I got to school, I was so distraught, I went straight to the nurse's office because I felt "sick." My hair fell out significantly due to me trying to straighten my Jheri curl.

Reflecting on this situation, how did I think my mom would not notice? She would have to figure out how to fix the issue I caused. Because I surely had no idea how to take care of it. If it was up to me, I would have stayed home from school until my hair grew back. Well, that was not an option. My mom doing what most parents and caregivers do, she took care of the problem.

"My mom doing what most parents and caregivers do, she took care of the problem."

There was a stylist named Shorty. He lived on Sheffield Street in Manchester and had a full salon in his basement. I remember the vivid smell of relaxers, Jheri curl spray, burning hair and a variety of food in his basement. At my first appointment with Shorty I remember him saying he was going to cut my hair some more because it was damaged. He said he would have to cut it so that he could get rid of the damaged hair and my hair would be able to grow in healthy. I immediately started crying, I mean literally crying. Here I was at this salon with this man who was supposed to be one of the best in Pittsburgh at what he does, and he was about to make my hair worse! To top it off his solution of a hairstyle was finger waves, finger waves, what? I was 12 years old with like 1 ½ inches of hair, how in the world was I supposed to have finger waves. He might as well have said he was going to give me a church boy haircut. I could not understand it and I just knew it would not play out well once I got home and back to school. But I had no choice.

Once he cut all the processed hair out, that left me with little to work with. He then processed the "virgin" hair that was remaining and gave me finger waves. Every grown person in that shop told me how "sharp" my hair was. Ummmmm, ma'am, I am all of 12 years old, I do not want to have a "sharp" hairstyle. I wanted them to say it was fly or bad. But not sharp! Nonetheless me, my mom and my "sharp" hairstyle took the bus back to the Hill.

I continued to get my hair done by Shorty for almost a year. My hair began growing back, and I was glad to move on from the 1 ½ inch finger waves.

I remember when I was in the 6th grade, I missed so much school due to being "sick" that the doctors thought I had gastritis. Gastritis is an inflammation, irritation or erosion of the lining of the stomach. The reason they thought it was gastritis is because every time I went to see the school nurse, was sent home or went to the pediatrician it was for a stomachache. A stomachache that never produced vomit or diarrhea, just a stomachache.

At the age of 12, I had to have a tube put down my throat into my stomach to check for this condition. I think I knew there was nothing medically wrong with me, but I could not say I am being picked on, so I do not want to be in school and the only true unidentified illness is a stomachache. So, I had to fully commit to the procedure. After this traumatizing procedure I found out I did not have gastritis. Just a case of being bullied and low self-esteem.

"I chose to press forward."

At a young age, I had to decide if I would allow my situation to continue affecting me in a negative way or press forward and embrace who God created. I chose to press forward. Yes, at the age of 12, I made this life-changing decision. I knew an entire year before I graduated Middle School that I would not be going to the High School that most people in my neighborhood attended.

I made a conscious decision to change my surroundings. This decision did not happen without harboring resentments and extreme defensiveness. Although I chose not to allow those things to "bother" me anymore, I was still angry and had intense dislike for those who I felt harmed me. Often, we think we have dealt with an issue because it did not kill us or physically destroy us. We say things like, "I am still standing." The question becomes how firm are you standing and are you really weighted by unresolved and unaddressed issues?

It is amazing to me the things that I was ashamed of and stressed over as a young person. These are the same things that I embrace as an adult. I was ashamed of my kinky hair, now my hair is chemical free, I considered bleaching cream and makeup as a young person, now I only wear make up for very special occasions unless its mascara or lipstick and my skin is not bleached.

I have been through my own personal cycles of life. It truly took the love, comfort and saving grace of God for me to appreciate me and my experiences. Through all the hurt, disappointments, fears, suicidal thoughts, lonely nights and tear-filled eyes (my own agitation during my washing), I have come to love me and others!

"I have been through my own personal cycles of life."

Young Adult Stains

As a young adult, I was so dirty and unwashed. My issues had completely consumed me. I had so many unresolved issues in my life that began to surface and corrupt me, mentally, physically and emotionally. If you noticed I did not say spiritually because I had no spiritual connection to God. I believed in God. I attended church at times and even asked for His help, often. I was using God as my personal genie in a bottle. This is not a bad thing; it is just where I was with my relationship to God. I think often people are criticized for their relationship or lack of relationship with God, but no one knows the work He is doing in them and where the relationship potentially will grow to become.

Although I attended church, prayed, begged, cried and pleaded at times, I did not have a relationship with God. The relationship simply was not present in my life. In a relationship there is a connection and inclusion in your personal life. God was not included in my personal life; well He was included on a very conditional basis. I called on Him, when I needed something or messed something up. I did not pray to Him often or talk to Him with gratitude for the grace shown to me for things that I did not deserve or His mercy for keeping things away from me that should have come my way. I never truly expressed gratitude for being spared and covered by God.

". . . people are criticized for their relationship or lack of relationship with God, but no one knows the work He is doing in them . . ."

The relationship with God was very one sided, I call, He answers. Everything else I kept Him out of. He was not included in my daily life decisions. Imagine being in relationship with someone and they only come around, call, text, email, etc. when they need something. How would you feel? I know I would feel used and think the relationship was not a healthy one. I had many issues that I was facing, and it took me a long time to develop a personal relationship with God. I am grateful for growth and understanding.

My young adulthood was extremely stressful. I was struggling at all ends. Most times I did not know if I was coming or going. I felt myself broken all the way down. My relationship with my children suffered. It took me a long time to admit this. I thought the things I was doing to make my children's lives better was for them. I thought if I worked hard and try to shield them from certain things and people, they would not experience some of the things that I experienced. I thought, get a "good job," be conscious about where you choose to live, where they attend school and do not intentionally expose them to negative situations. All of these moves I was making came at a cost. I was a preoccupied parent. Through all of this I could not grasp that I had absolutely no balance at all and I was bottling up everything I was running from or trying to bury.

This revelation of being a preoccupied parent came to me during a sermon that my pastor preached in September of 2017. One of Pastor Edmonds' five points for that day was The Preoccupied Parent, in which he referenced parents not being present and the success of a child being related to this. I had to admit to myself that my lack of presence impacted my children. Children need their parents, not just things from their parents. My daughter, Nia, recently said to me, "I would like to be able to come to you for more than just stuff that I need. I need physical and EMOTIONAL SUPPORT." Yes, she sent a text with emotional support in all caps. She is my child. The point is she was letting me know that she appreciated the "things" and that I made sure her tangible needs were met, but she had other needs as well. Needs that help a person develop into a well-rounded adult. At different points of my life, both my children have expressed this to me, but in very different ways. Hassan is a bit blunter, as he is my child also and often referenced me not attending events or said, "I guess you are going to be asleep?"

Although I had my reasons, and I believed they were positive, my preoccupation had an impact on my children. I admit I was not present in the way that I needed to be. It has taken me some time to forgive myself for this. I can see the damage my preoccupation has caused or at least contributed to. I am grateful that through my relationship with God, healing is happening now, and our relationship is being repaired.

Like other points of my life I recognized that something was wrong. What was that thing or things? I did not relate it to my unresolved issues. I did not make the correlation between repeat behaviors and the fact that I had not dealt with anxiety, low self-esteem, past depression, trauma, etc.

I thought I was pressing forward because I was not focusing on those unresolved issues. I thought the negative things were behind me because I was having positive experiences in my life. But God said, "Wait a minute!" I was busy focusing on MY accomplishments that I had pressed all the negative feelings, and situations so far down they were now buried under my accomplishments. I convinced myself that the accomplishments were for my children, but they were largely for me. There was a part of me that unconsciously needed to feel accomplished. The things that I experienced as a young person felt defeating. I needed a win. But what I did not realize is my children needed me to be present more than be accomplished. There is a thin line that single parents/caregivers must walk and attempt to do so carefully. We want what is best for our children so much that we often sacrifice essential parts of our relationship with them. I do not believe that we do this with malice. Although I thought I had buried these negative things they were slowly beginning to surface and those closest to me suffered. I tried so hard to mask and bury the past, but God had other plans.

It was the year 2000, and I was at my churches' Women's Conference. This would prove to be an experience unlike any other. In preparation for the conference we had a "shut in." I thought, "What in the

WORLD?" But I went along with it and we remained awake at the church all night in prayer, seeking God, asking for Him to be present and have His way.
The first day of the conference I was in a small group morning session. I witnessed people being "slain in the spirit." My immediate reaction was rolling my eyes, sucking my teeth, criticizing and doubting their experience. I thought, it does not take all of that and the minister is just pushing them down. In hindsight, I realize people were experiencing exactly what we had been praying for all night, for God to have his way.

At 7 pm we gathered in the main sanctuary for the evening service. I was seated on the main level in the center section. During praise and worship I was uneasy but still felt good. I was standing with my hands lifted, eyes closed, and tears streaming down my face. The minister stood at the podium for prayer and said, "There is someone here struggling with suicide." I knew it was me but did not want to acknowledge it. She said it a couple more times and then I hear her say, "Is it you?" I opened my eyes and her eyes were piercing my soul. Now mind you, there were several hundred women present. She told me to come out into the aisle. The aisle, of the main sanctuary, during the main event of the night. I stepped out and she came down, laid hands on me and prayed. In her prayer she let me know that I did not want to commit suicide, I just wanted rest. I went down! Yes, me I WENT DOWN! When I opened my eyes, my aunt was kneeling over me crying. I got up went to the bathroom to gather myself. I came back to my seat and knew I had been delivered. I knew those thoughts would be no more. In that moment God showed me that when He intends for harmful things to be removed you have no choice but to obey and it will be by any means necessary.

In that moment I was completely open to the change that was needed. I had been trying to suppress my hurts and past ills, and God said ENOUGH! He knew what I was really dealing with behind closed doors, in the middle of the night when no one else was around. He knew I would lay in my bed and cry like a baby, cry until I had a headache and cry myself to sleep many nights. He knew how it was impacting not only me, but my children. God's initial intention was for me to be delivered from my thoughts of suicide in an intimate setting. I chose to use that opportunity during the day sessions to watch and judge others. I was accusing them of faking. This was my own defense against being vulnerable and open to the healing that was needed. He knew that committing suicide would be taking away the sanctity of life, the fullness of life promised to us by God. In my case they were negative thoughts which could have become actions. God chose "prime time" and location to remind me that He is God. If he says it is so, then it is so.

That experience and releasing those suicidal thoughts was so freeing. All these things in my past and present, emotionally, mentally, and physically that were causing those suicidal thoughts were released all at once and a spiritual connection was established. I still have trials and tribulations, but because of God I have learned to deal with them differently and not consider squandering the precious life that I have been afforded. God Loves us and desires for us to experience the fullness of what He has for us.

AUTHOR'S REFLECTION

I think it is important to not only acknowledge that people struggle with thoughts of suicide, but suicide does not have a specific look. When I was at my lowest point, there were people close to me who did not know. I am not certain why, but it was a shock for them to realize I had thoughts of suicide. Although a person may not look like they are having thoughts of taking their own life, it is important when we know that they have a full plate that we at least check in to ask how they are doing. A full plate could be different for each person. When I reference a full plate, I mean managing multiple responsibilities at the same time.

Often a person who is responsible for multiple things at the same time, children, work, school, spouse, church, family, friends, etc., they spend very little time actively partaking in self-care. In addition, this person may have also experienced the loss of those things mentioned such as, employment, housing, family, friends, etc., this can lead to feelings of defeat. All of this may make them feel like they no longer want to deal with the responsibilities, challenges or disappointments of life.

If a person has expressed feelings of sadness or struggles of dealing with life in general, do not ignore those things or say, "Yeah we all have stuff going on." Although this is true, not everyone can break through those trials the same. Take time to see beyond the person's "look."

If a person has expressed feelings of sadness or struggles of dealing with life in general, do not ignore those things or say,
"Yeah we all have stuff going on."

PART II
Internal Cleansing

The Internal Cleansing Process

Mind

Body

Spirit

In the beginning of the book I spoke about being unclean. My lack of cleanliness was not external — not my skin, my hair, my nails, etc. It was about being unclean internally. I am referring to the dirt and soil that takes a good scrubbing. You can go through life cleaning the outside only. To be honest, some of us "clean up" pretty good. But that internal cleaning is a whole different story. That is the dirt that you cannot fake getting rid of because it is within you and you take you wherever you go!

"My lack of cleanliness was not external — not my skin, my hair, my nails, etc. It was about being unclean internally."

I am referencing my actual being, the fabric of who I am, my true self, and struggles.

Let us look at fabric and how it is cleaned. The cleaning cannot just take place on the surface. You must get down to the inner pieces of the material's fiber. Get down deep to the actual structure that weaves it all together. It is an intimate process; you must go beyond the surface. Go beyond that top layer, scrub a bit and maybe even deep clean.

Dirt goes deep! It gets intertwined into the very minutiae pieces of fiber and the fiber of who we are. When you begin working on who you are and go beyond the surface you will experience things that you never imagined. I am not just talking about tangible things that you can touch, such as cars, houses, jewelry, etc. I am talking about life sustaining things such as peace, joy, and unconditional love for self and others.

The correlation between doing laundry and internal cleaning of self:

CHAPTER 1 DIRTY CLOTHES HAMPER	Contains your Mind, Body, Spirit
CHAPTER 2 SORT CLOTHING	Identify past, present trauma, mental health issues, drug and alcohol issues, hurts, familial discord, grief, disappointments, loss, etc.
CHAPTER 3 PREPARATION	Choose what will work best for you; choose a cleaning agent that is not too harsh, but strong enough to cleanse your issues.
ADD DETERGENT	Now that you have chosen your cleaning agent it is time to add it to the process.
LOAD THE WASHER	Acknowledge, accept, and commit to address issues
SELECT WATER TEMPERATURE	How deep are the stains and how delicate are your issues and concerns? Do your concerns need the attention of the extreme temperatures either hot or cold? Are your stains mild? Can warm water address them?
SELECT THE CYCLE	How fast do you want to address or resolve your issues?

PRE-SOAK	Some things impact us differently. Your issues may need extra care and attention depending on how deep they are and how long they have been left unattended.
CHAPTER 4 **HIT START**	Begin to discuss or address your issues. This can be done with a traditional therapist, spiritual leader, accountability partner, friend, family member, support person, physical activity, or a quiet conversation with you and God. Understanding that different issues and experiences may need more than one avenue to address the situation and begin the cleansing and healing process.
CHAPTER 5 **AGITATION**	You will feel irritated and things that you thought were behind you will creep back in. You may feel like the work is not worth it, the sacrifice is not worth it, the pain and pressure of dealing with these issues is not worth it, but do not give up! This is part of the process.
CHAPTER 6 **RINSE CYCLE**	Some of the issues that you are adding the cleaning agent to are beginning to be washed away. The water is needed, you are not drowning in your issues you are being purified and being rid of those undesirable things.

It may feel like you are not making progress and things are not getting better. You may feel like your head is spinning, your emotions are everywhere, your relationship and trust in God is uncertain. Just know that this is also part of the process. You are almost there! When this process is done the unwanted stains of life will be gone and floating down a drain. They will no longer be attainable unless you dig into the muck and mire of the sewage looking for them again.

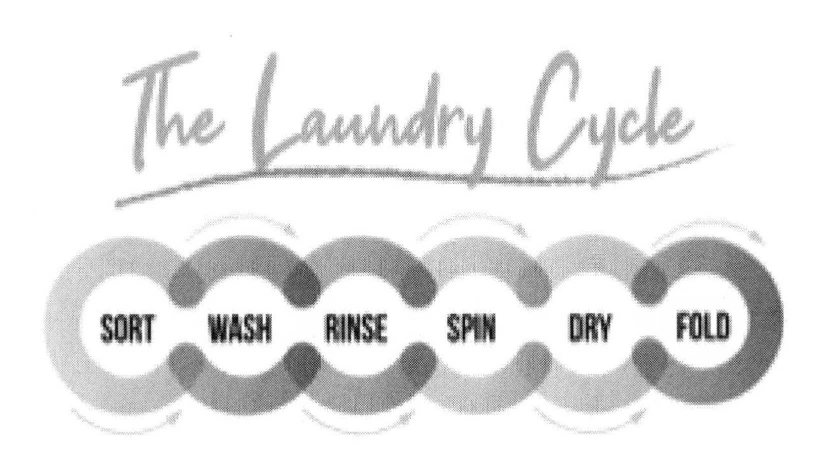
The Laundry Cycle
SORT
WASH
RINSE
SPIN
DRY
FOLD

Chapter 1
The Dirty Clothes Hamper
Those Internal Things

When my children were younger, laundry was such a task. They had clothes for preschool, play clothes, "play- play" clothes (you know those are the clothes that are too small with unrepairable damage). They had extra clothes that we kept in the cubby just in case they had an accident or spilled an unrecognizable meal while eating. It seemed like my life's mission was to complete the task of laundry. This was a never-ending task!

Laundry time was not a romantic meet up by any stretch of the imagination. I did not receive a sexy call from a guy name Sir Laundry who asked, "What are you doing Saturday evening? How about we spend some alone time together? I did not have a date and time set on the calendar that me and the dirty clothes, fabric softener, bleach, and detergent would get together for some "alone "time." Secretly I wished for a "date" because the alone time with the laundry was overrated. Laundry was a task that could not be ignored. There were many signs that it was time to take care of it.

My life was not set up to have scheduled time for much, certainly not laundry. If it was not about the basic needs (food, clothing, shelter), I did not have the mental or emotional capacity to consistently complete it. Those things that I did not think played a major role in the end game to obtain basic needs were put on the back burner until I could address them. I was living a true "means to an end" lifestyle. I was going through each day completing tasks to reach a goal without a purpose.

This was my life and completing the task of laundry did not rank that high on the list. I did it because I knew it had to be done, but it was usually when it was time to take garbage bags full to the laundry and put them in the triple loader. There was always a clear sign that it was time to do my laundry.

I DO NOT LIKE WHAT I SEE

When your dirty clothes are piled up and your hamper is overflowing you know it is time to do your laundry. If you were to continue to pile dirty clothes on top of dirty clothes, eventually a stench will begin to permeate throughout your house. Have you ever entered a room and a horrible smell hits you square in the face? You make the stank face, your eyes squint, your nose and mouth meet and your eyebrows frown. Depending on the severity of the smell your nose and eyes may burn. Yes, the stench could be that real.

If you allow dirty clothes to continue to go unattended, the effects of the dirt and other grimy substances that rested on those clothes will become overwhelming. Besides the smell, the other substances resting on the fabric of the clothes will possibly ruin the fabric. Even when you eventually address the awful stench and stains, it is important to be mindful that there may be a light faded mark where the stain rested for so long, but this does not mean the fabric is completely ruined. The fabric may still have a purpose.

There are many reasons that stains may show up on your clothes. Notice I said, "show up" because there are times I literally look down on my clothes and wonder where and when did this happen. Perhaps you brush up against a dirty car or a cute little child touches you with melted chocolate on their hands. Maybe a pen explodes on your shirt. Maybe while driving to a meeting and eating a juicy burger with the works the contents spill out and ruin your white dress, ok maybe this last one is just me. However stains occur, they will eventually need addressed or the article of clothing can be ruined permanently. Both a stench and stain will damage the fabric of clothing. Think about it, when you damage something it changes the value.

There is a rug called the Red Tabriz Persian Rug, and it costs about $35,000. If you were to spill grape juice on this rug you will surely devalue the rug because it is now damaged. This rug is very expensive, but the value of your life is priceless. Therefore, it is imperative that you think about the stains on material fabric in correlation with the fabric of you as a person. You are the person that God has literally woven together. Every fiber of your being was chosen by God to weave together and create you. There was deliberate thought and purpose to your creation. You are invaluable! You have every right to preserve you, and with great intention care for your personal fabric.

YOU MATTER

Take a minute to think about the stains in your life. Those marks, blemishes, or smears that can and have been damaging. Those situations and relationships in your life that may have or currently are taking a toll on you. The circumstances that without any deep thought, kill your joy, that cause you to frown your face, crinkle your eyebrows. The divorce, the abusive relationship, the discord with family and friends, the addiction, the anxiety, the depression, the low self-esteem, the trauma, the molestation, the body image issues, the grief, the loss, and the suicidal thoughts. The list can go on and on, as we all have encountered situations in our lives that have stained us in some way. If we go through our lives without addressing these stains, if we choose not to seek help, or support for these stains in our lives, like an article of clothing we could be damaged forever. Those things will sit in a pile and progressively get worse. Even if no one knows how damaging our experiences were or currently are, we know and there will always be a faded stain present. We can mask it by dressing up the outside. I am not only referring to dressing up with clothing, but with our speech. You know the articulate one, and if you do not, I do. I am her. At times I am so articulate, I forget I have issues that I really need to address instead of spending time dominating conversations.

We dress up with our social circles, our cars, our homes, our business relationships, the boards we sit on, the list goes on. The reality is if there are unaddressed stains in our lives those things will eventually take a back seat because the stench will begin to become present. The stench from within that develops is much like the unaddressed article of clothing. What happens when something has a stench? When a stench is present people do not want to be near it. At times it will make people ill. I remember going to a local variety store with my cousin and the moment I entered the store an overwhelming stench hit me in my face! I was so disgusted. I began asking the people in the store, "You don't smell that?" I grabbed the items out of my cousin's hand and told her that she would not be purchasing anything from that store. That smell was so strong that it had no other choice but to latch onto her and the items that had been sitting on the shelves. I was convinced if we stayed in the presence of that stench for much longer, we would leave with it. Then it would be our problem.

If we do not address the stains in our lives and the stench that develops, people will not want to be around us. They will not want to engage us with the attitude or disposition we may have. Just like a stench in clothing that you can smell before you identify it, that is how your presence will be. People will smell you coming!

Notice I said we, yes, I am including myself in the conversation. I have dirty laundry, too. I had to identify those things in my life, past and present, that play a role in damaging my fabric. I had to accept that things happened, but through prayer and relationship with God they could become a work in progress and even deliverance is possible. I recognize I am not the person that I would like to be. I still have some stains and stench that I am working to treat. I also recognize, much like the fabric that has a stain or stench, that treating it is an option. I had to work on loving and appreciating myself enough to address those stains, begin to separate from other stenches and move on to cleaner fabrics with healthy aromas.

Just as stains on fabric need to be addressed the stains (hurts and resentments) in our lives need to be addressed.

Just as stains on fabric need to be addressed the stains (hurts and resentments) in our lives need to be addressed. If you were hurt in a past relationship you cannot just "move on" to the next. That past relationship that caused hurt has damaged you (your fabric). It may have damaged you physically, mentally, spiritually and/or emotionally. Therefore, the healing will need to occur to restore your fabric or at least begin to treat it. Restoration may not be in full but by addressing and continuously caring for the issue you will have lessened the damage.

CHAPTER 1 REFLECTION
THINK ABOUT IT

Identify stains in your life that you need to address.

____

____

____

____

____

Have these identified life stains damaged your personal fabric? Yes ☐ No ☐
If yes, how?

____

____

____

____

____

Are any of your life stains personal resentments?
Yes ☐ No ☐
If yes, identify your resentments.

____

____

____

____

____

Chapter 2
Sorting

Not all things are created equal!

During this step in the process it is important to realize how properly sorting will impact the outcome.

Identify past, present trauma, mental health issues, drug and alcohol issues, hurts, familial discord, grief, disappointments, loss, etc. Take the necessary time to sort these things. Some may have had more impact than others and need to be placed into a separate pile.

INTERNAL SORTING

Once you have acknowledged that your laundry will need attention, you now must sort the clothes. You cannot take all the clothes out of the hamper and put them in the washing machine. The load may be too heavy or have too many different colors or too many fabric types in the identified load. Sorting the dirty clothes into piles is a chore and you must pay attention to the process. Do not forget to empty pockets. Items that are hidden may cause a lot of damage.

Let us sit here for one minute. Often, it is the hidden things that may cause the most damage. Have you ever left a writing pen or piece of candy in your pocket during the laundry process? If you have, then you know that damage can occur, and it was not only to the article of clothing that the hidden item impacted. It also may have caused some damage to those other items that you were attempting to get clean as well. If it was a writing pen, then the ink spread and if it was a piece of candy the sugar once wet and melted, may have stuck to other articles of clothing.

Think about the people or responsibilities in your life. When you are going through your cleaning process and you do not clear the way of those "hidden issues" you begin to impact those things around you. The people you encounter, the responsibilities on your job or within social or spiritual settings begin to be impacted because those hidden things spill out one way or another.

What should you consider when sorting your laundry?

- Similar Colors (Identified Issues and Concerns)

    - Keep your light and dark clothes separate. There are different levels of severity of your identified issues and concerns. You cannot mix all your experiences, hurts, trauma, resentments, and disappointments together.
- Various care needs (Some issues and concerns are more sensitive and have a little more dirt)
    - Do not mix undergarments and other articles or clothing. Undergarments need extra special attention.
    - Possible bleeding or shrinkage
        - Think about the damage that these two things can cause and the possibility that you will not be able to enjoy the article of clothing as you once did.
- Size of load (You cannot handle everything at once.)
    - Make sure the size of the load is appropriate for the machine's capacity level.
    - Make sure the water and laundry detergent can properly circulate. Each article of clothing must receive attention. You are the article of clothing (the fabric). The article of clothing must have the opportunity to go through the process and be cleaned.

It is important to know that you need to take an active role in your own personal healing. You need to put yourself first, you need to identify those things that have adversely impacted you. Remain committed to the process. Take time to acknowledge and celebrate each milestone while healing. These are just a few needs, and things that you cannot take lightly.

"It is important to know that you need to take an active role in your own personal healing."

Sorting is also important because:

- Integrity is preserved
    - Why is integrity important? Integrity speaks to who you are at your core, your principles, your honesty. Integrity is worth preserving.
- Address and avoid generational issues
    - Those so-called generational curses. I am a firm believer that these such things can indeed be broken.
- Allows you to identify what can be most harmful and what can be helpful
    - Everything cannot be cleaned together and at the same time. Your clothing may be damaged if you combine various clothing.
- Allows you to Prioritize
    - Not all things are created equal

PRESERVING INTEGRITY

Integrity is defined as the quality of being honest and having strong moral principles; moral uprightness. How do you view integrity? Does integrity have any value in your life? Do you think that it is relevant to who you are? When I think of integrity I think of honesty. I think of integrity as the foundation of who I am and what I believe. My integrity is no longer something that I am willing to compromise. Do I still make mistakes? Of course, because no one is perfect. To answer my questions above, yes, I think integrity adds value to my life. Yes, I think it is relevant to who I am. But in the spirit of this book I must be honest and say there were times in my life that I compromised my integrity. I was involved in relationships, not all intimate, some were friendships that were not in line with who I am at my core. I compromised my integrity. I would never say that someone else was responsible for my actions or behaviors, because I know me. I know what I stand for. I know how I was raised and who I am, each fiber. I knew what I should and should not have engaged in.

Yes, there were times that I was not necessarily thinking clear and my emotions were intense, intense enough to cloud rational judgement. But I still knew who I was at my core. Although, it was a hard pill to swallow I needed to be honest with myself and admit that I was behaving or engaging in situations that did not put me in the light of what God intends for me. To be clear, this is not a statement of, "having arrived" or perfection. I will admit I have a very long way to go. I am still in a process. Although I have overcome some things and been cleansed of some things, I am a work in progress. In this process I had to tap into my core and examine how to preserve my integrity instead of a process of continually chipping away at it.

As different issues began to compound, I realized I was losing more and more of who I was, my authentic me. I began to feel an internal breakdown. I understood there were a lot of things I needed to address, and cleansing was necessary, but I also realized it could not all be done together. To preserve the integrity of who I am I had to separate my different issues. I needed to do my absolute best to not allow one issue to bleed onto another or I would be in a perpetual cleansing cycle. I would never feel as if anything was being accomplished. I would feel like I was on a never-ending spin cycle.

I have a true desire to be the woman that God intends for me to be. Although some things have been compromised, I know enough to not allow complete destruction, death. I am not speaking of death in the physical sense, but spiritual death. I know I have something to still hold onto that will breathe into me and give me a new life, if I could just reach back and awaken my seemingly lost integrity.

GENERATIONAL ISSUES

The dreadful generational curse. We often hear people say a generational curse must be broken. My personal belief is that yes, there are experiences that are relative, but I am not of the mindset that anyone should subscribe to the idea of a generational curse. Holding negative and harmful situations is holding yourself hostage to the "what ifs" of life. Although the experiences are relevant to how your life has been shaped thus far, they do not have to define you or your future.

When sorting your issues, past, present trauma, mental health issues, drug and alcohol issues, hurts, familial discord, grief, disappointments, loss, etc., take a moment to analyze how long these things have been in existence.

Questions you may ask:

Has the stain reached the core of who I am?
Yes ☐ No ☐

Has this long-standing stain in my life started damaging who I am as a person?
Yes ☐ No ☐

Have I tried to rid myself of this stain?
Yes ☐ No ☐

If you answered yes to all or any of these questions, then it is imperative you look at the generational relevance to your issues.

WHAT IS THE DEPTH OF THE STAIN?

For instance, you notice an unknown laundry stain on a linen pant suit. You were aware but did not address the stain immediately. You tossed the suit in the back of your closet with true intentions of taking it to the cleaners. But time goes on, and you forget to have the suit cleaned.

Take a moment to think about that. How often are we aware of issues and do not address them immediately? We see the issue, we know it may be getting worse and we are aware that it will need attention, but we delay the process. Even though we are aware that if not addressed immediately the issue may get worse. The longer the stain rests on the fabric, the deeper it can become and the more damage it can cause. It is important to consider the depth because that is going to determine the level of intensity that will be needed to rid or lessen the impact of the stain on your fabric.

Has this long-standing stain in your life started damaging who you are?

When you are a child, you are in an environment that is not within your control. There are behaviors and traditions that may not be healthy or good for you as a person. Although these behaviors may be acceptable amongst your family and have become generational, they may not be healthy and soon become an issue.

In some families drinking is acceptable, even for young people. Some people will not think twice about telling a child to get them a beer from the refrigerator and then allowing that child to "take a swig" of the beer. This behavior may continue throughout the child's adolescent years until they themselves acquire a taste for beer. Eventually it can progress to more than an acquired taste for beer, but a true desire and need for beer or possibly additional addictive substances, such as liquor or illicit drugs. This seemingly innocent behavior of the family at a child's young age can have a lasting impact on the child and cause a stain/issue of addiction.

This is a very serious issue and will need to be separated from some other things that you are going to cleanse that are having a negative impact on your life. This issue is complex because it is not just about you, but the familial dynamics that contributed to the issue. It will be imperative that you truly evaluate how harmful this issue is and has been in your life.

Have you ever tried to rid yourself of this stain?

Although it may be hard, because change and growth are often a little difficult, but have you tried to address those stains in your life? The uncomfortable feeling cannot be a deterrent to addressing the stains in your life because it is necessary to help you become a healthier and joyous you! Understanding the stains that are generational may not have been created by you, but they are impacting you. The importance of trying to rid yourself of those generational stains is truly to help you and not others. Often, we choose not to address generational stains because of how the conversations and actions will impact others, but this is a time to be selfish. This is difficult, but again necessary. For some of us giving of ourselves at the expense of ourselves comes naturally. We take on hurts and pains created by others in our attempt to save and preserve relationships.

Although helping others may leave you with a warm and fuzzy feeling inside, that is not what you need at this time. It is time to help yourself.

HARMFUL

Another aspect of sorting is making sure you keep all things that have been more harmful than others with their likeness. Many times, instructions on the labels of clothing instruct you to wash with like colors. The reason is some clothing may bleed onto others. Another reason is because some articles of clothing may be delicate and others such as jeans may be stronger.

Previously in the section **"Has this long-standing stain in your life started damaging who you are?"** I mentioned a scenario of how addiction may develop. Take a closer look at this issue and how it relates to this section of sorting and deciding what is harmful. The issue of addiction was essentially orchestrated and facilitated by the older people charged to care for this child. We will call her Lisa. Because of Lisa's experience as a child and not feeling protected or guided in a positive direction there may be strained relationships, resentment, anger, sadness, hurt and/or anxiety currently in Lisa's adult life.

Consider this Scenario:

As a young person a friendship developed in high school with a neighbor, Anna. Lisa became very close to Anna, almost like family. As young adults, Lisa and Anna had a disagreement with each other, and communication ceased. The disagreement greatly impacted their friendship. Years later, Lisa began thinking about Anna and how much she missed their friendship. She struggled to remember why they had a disagreement. We have all had this happen, so much time passes by you cannot remember why you were upset. You can only remember how you feel, but not many details about the disagreement. Lisa decides she is going to be the "mature one" and reach out to Anna to have a discussion. Lisa is hoping she can reopen the lines of communication, address past hurts, and hopefully move on to a renewed healthy friendship. During the conversation their voices become raised and Lisa begins to accuse Anna of being a disappointment and stating that she felt abandoned by Anna. Anna is dumbfounded! It becomes clear that Lisa is speaking from a place of hurt stemming from her familial history and not her friend.

Essentially what Lisa did was dump her familial issues and expectations onto Anna. The issues may have been similar but not to the same magnitude or level of expectation. Her friend did not have the same responsibility as her family. The harm that was caused by the actions of her family was different than that of the disagreement with her friend.

Often, we lump all our hurt together and like a snow plow we push it at the same time to the same destination. The reality is we must prioritize our issues so that we do not negatively impact and harm other relationships.

PRIORITIZING

Prioritizing allows you to evaluate what issues have had the most impact and the level of immediacy. This is extremely helpful in the cleansing process. Think about it, if you have several things that you need to accomplish for the week all of them may need to get done, but if not completed, some may have more of an adverse impact than others. For instance, as you are preparing to do your laundry you begin the sorting process. While doing this you see that you have items with stains that appear to be ingrained in the fabric. These are items you may not have noticed. Once you notice it, then it becomes a priority.

You should address these items first because the potential for future or irrevocable damage is present. When we prioritize, it also helps us to stay organized and complete goals. If your goal is to become well and live life to the fullest, then prioritize how to achieve these goals. For instance, **your priority may be** *to address generational stains that have negatively impacted your life* and **your goal may be** *to maintain healthy relationships.*

When we prioritize, it also helps us to stay organized and complete goals.

Here are a few questions in prioritizing and setting goals that you should consider:

How and for how long have these stains impacted your life?

____

____

____

____

____

How have you suffered loss of self-worth because of these stains?

____

____

____

____

____

How extensive is the damage? Has it passed onto others through your actions or inaction? For example, relationships with your children, significant other, work or your social life.

____

____

____

____

____

CHAPTER 2 REFLECTION
THINK ABOUT IT

Identify the different piles of concerns in your life, understanding that everything cannot go into the same load at the same time. List your "piles."

___

___

___

___

___

Look at the individual past or present trauma, abuse, hurts, familial discord, mental health, addiction, etc. List your individual concerns.

___

___

___

___

___

Take a minute to sort your concerns. What will you address first? Is it possible to address multiple concerns at the same time?

___

___

___

___

___

Chapter 3
Preparation

Get ready to address your issues, hurts, things that have contributed to your brokenness

Preparation — Choose a cleaning agent that is not too harsh, but strong enough to cleanse your issues.

Add Detergent — Now that you have chosen your cleaning agent it is time to add it to the process.

Load the Washer — Acknowledge, accept, and commit to address issues

Select Water Temperature — How deep are the stains and how delicate are your issues and concerns?

Select the Cycle — How fast do you want to address or resolve your issues?

Pre-Soak —Your issues may need extra care and attention depending on how deep they are and how long they have been left unattended.

CHOOSING YOUR CLEANING AGENT/DETERGENT

Now that you have sorted your clothes you must choose a detergent, or cleaning agent. This is an absolute necessity. Because your clothes will not be cleaned without it. Much like when you choose a cleaning agent for addressing the dirt with your clothing you need to do the same when it comes to confronting your unaddressed issues and concerns in your life.

People have chosen many cleaning agents to help them heal and navigate through life. Some have chosen a therapist, family, friends, support groups, mentors, church family, preachers, priests, and physical activities, etc.

As for me, I have utilized all the above, but my favorite cleansing agent has been my alone time with God. He sees us. He hears us. He desires for us to be clean. Just like you desire for your clothes to be cleaned, God wants the same for us, the fabric that He created. He desires for us to be clean and made whole. Even when I am surrounded by others, I am often having alone time with God. My relationship with God has developed over time.

As a young adult, I remember unconsciously searching for mental and emotional refuge. I knew I needed support and an outlet to help me manage the mental and emotional chaos that I was experiencing. However, I was uncertain where to go or who to turn to. One thing I was sure of was that it was not healthy to face it alone. I wanted to be whole. I wanted to empty out those negative and harmful thoughts and be filled up with positivity and a healthy mind. My process included therapy, family, friends, support groups, mentors, church family and preachers.

All of which played an essential part in my progress. They all functioned as cleaning agents to support and guide me through the circumstances I was experiencing. Ultimately, I began my consistent journey with God, and He has been my cleaning agent ever since. I am grateful for the support and impact of those other agents in my life and they have each led me to a better understanding of self.

LOAD THE WASHER

Now is the time that you are to acknowledge, accept and commit to address your issues. Remember this is just one load. As you load the washer be sure not to "stuff" the entire load in at once. What happens when something is stuffed? The item that is holding those things may lose its shape, become damaged, some of the items that it was intended to hold may fall out. Imagine if this happened to you as a person. What if you separated all your issues, hurts, things that have contributed to your brokenness to be addressed individually, only to then decide to stuff them all into one healing session. The purpose of cleansing oneself is to give the proper time, space, and attention to each concern. If you load all your issues at once, the purpose and integrity may be lost.

Take each article of clothing and place it in the washer. Remember each piece of clothing will need to receive attention through the process or some items may come out unclean.

SELECT WATER TEMPERATURE

Before selecting the cycle, you must choose the water temperature. When cleansing your fabric, it is important to choose the "right" temperature. The temperature that you choose is not meant to make you feel comfortable, but to heal, cleanse, and address your issues.

DIFFERENCE IN WATER TEMPERATURES

Cold Water is meant to avoid or lessen the risk of shrinking or the colors from fading. Often, delicate clothes are washed in cold water. When we have delicate issues in our life, we want to be sure to handle them carefully. Many times, people expect that when going through a healing/cleansing process issues should be addressed quickly and forgotten. If I had a dollar for every time someone said just address it, deal with it, and move on, I would be rich. It is not always that easy and we should be mindful when going through our own process or supporting others that it is a process and should be handled as such.

Warm Water is meant to achieve cleanliness without using extremes (cold or hot water). Warm water cannot remove heavy soils and stains. There are stains in your life that do not require extreme attention. These stains have had an impact and addressing them will allow you to grow and become a better person. You may not see them as things in your life that have an immediate impact. For instance, if you do not have serious health concerns, then losing weight and changing your eating habits may be something that can be addressed with warm water. You recognize problems may arise if not addressed, but at this point the issues are not severe enough that they require extreme attention.

Hot Water is meant to tackle those clothes that need the most attention, not necessarily good attention. They are the clothes that have been through a lot, maybe under garments. The hot water will kill the germs. Hot water may be uncomfortable. It may appear that the hot water will harm you, but in the end, it may be what is needed to cleanse you and deal with the issues of your life that can cause further damage. Hot water is used to address garments that are deeply soiled, stains that may have been resting on the fabric for a while.

Think about some deep-seated issues that you have had for a long time in your life, perhaps since childhood. You cannot deal with those things delicately or from a middle ground. Often people find themselves in "hot water." This term has been used often as an indication that someone may be in trouble or that the situation, they are in may be uncomfortable or difficult to handle. The hot water you may find yourself in can be used to force you to make changes and make you stronger. The way you address these issues will have to be aggressive and you will need to "turn up the heat!"

SELECT THE CYCLE

The different laundry cycles are designed to provide specialized attention to the various articles of clothing that are placed in the washing machine.

THE NORMAL CYCLE

In a basic washing machine, the regular or normal cycle will create the longest cycle with the most agitation. For a soiled, dirty, sweaty typical load of clothes this is the cycle you want to choose.
The normal cycle often lasts anywhere from 8 to 15 minutes. This is the actual time the machine spends agitating the clothes to get them clean.

This cycle uses a 'fast/fast' combination, meaning the washing cycle is fast and the spin cycle is fast as well. Cottons and linens are fabrics that tolerate the normal cycle very well. They are sturdy fabrics that can withstand this degree of agitation and clothes become very clean as a result.

THE PERMANENT PRESS CYCLE

For many years, I just did not know what this cycle was used for. I now understand that it is **primarily used for synthetic fibers such as rayon, knits, polyesters and acetates.** These fabric materials need the agitation of the regular cycle, but the slow spin of the delicate cycle as to not wrinkle clothes.

The Permanent-Press cycle lasts on average from 7 to 10 minutes and uses a 'fast/slow' combination.

Permanent Press uses the vigorous speed of the actual washing cycle and uses a slow spin cycle. While the slow spin cycle does not extract as much water from the clothes, it does prevent a good amount of wrinkling. Synthetic fibers are known for harboring smells and they can only be removed by the agitation experienced

in a fast cycle. Synthetic fabrics are also known for pilling, and it is only increased with friction.
By choosing a slower spin cycle, it also helps decrease the wear and tear on the fabric, thus causing less pilling.

THE DELICATE CYCLE

The Delicate or Gentle cycle is the **most ambiguous** of the three. There is not necessarily a specific fabric that requires the delicate cycle (other than washable silk or wool), however **there are *many* reasons to use this cycle.**

The delicate cycle uses a 'slow/slow' combination, meaning that the wash cycle uses a slow or lesser degree of agitation and the spin cycle uses a slow spin to extract water from laundry.

A delicate cycle usually lasts between 4 and 7 minutes during its actual wash cycle. By using a 'slow/slow' cycle, the agitation and abrasion on the clothes is greatly reduced and offers a certain level of protection for some fabrics.

Again, there are a few fabrics that need the delicate cycle and there are specific garments that need the extra protection offered by the gentle cycle.

Also, items that have weak fibers such as antique pieces or lacy items need the extra protection of the gentle cycle.

The delicate cycle is **designed to be less abrasive, using less agitation**. So, while it provides less wear and tear on your clothes, it also decreases the level of clean in some instances. As stated above, each cycle selection (normal, permanent press and delicate) needs more substance in order to apply the process of addressing personal issues.

Each cycle has a purpose designed for the specific laundry stains an article of clothing may have. Be mindful of your life stains when choosing your cycle.

ADD CLEANING AGENT/ DETERGENT

The amount of detergent/cleaning agent that you add to your load is important. Please understand that during your process of cleansing you may be fragile. Some issues may be generational issues and you will need to consider how much you can take at one time. Remember this is a process, which means there is a series of actions to achieve a specific goal. Keeping this in mind, if you add too much detergent too soon there could be an adverse effect, which could impact your healing.

Some of the issues and concerns that you are dealing with may have taken some time to manifest. Take your time and make sure you do not treat it like the first jump into the pool on a hot summer day. That experience may be refreshing to your body but jumping in and "drowning" yourself with your chosen cleaning agent may not feel the same. Start slowly by putting your toes in first. For instance, you may decide that your healing and coping will come by way of physical activities, but you have never been to the gym. You have walked by one or seen advertisements on television but have never actually been inside and worked out. If you decide to join a fitness bootcamp and attend 5 out of 7 days a week for intense circuit training, you will feel every bit of it and that decision may prove to be too much for you. In some cases, you may decide you no longer want to pursue this method of healing and give up.

Often when we are trying to heal, we bypass steps or attempt to move through them very quickly. The adding of your cleaning agent is just as important as the other steps in your process. Be mindful that once you have added the cleaning agent you are ready to hit start because all mechanisms are now in place. Do not be afraid or ashamed to take time with yourself. This will be an intense process.

PRE-SOAK

Wait a minute!

Are you truly ready to be cleansed? There are times our issues and concerns are so deep and have such a long history of existence and impact in our lives that they may need to be presoaked. If we recognize that they need attention, we may need to "massage" them so to speak, let them sit for a minute. Some of our pain, hurt, and guilt may be so profound that just throwing them into the wash process may be more harmful than helpful. Although the goal is to be whole, give yourself a break if needed.

This process will require that you take a minute and become self-aware to know if you need to approach a certain situation of healing more gingerly than others.

Think about the depth of the hurt and the length of time that the issue has existed. Self-inventory and reflection will be a must. Was the issue self-inflicted? Are others involved? If so, what is their relationship to you? Is your heart connected to those other people? All these questions should be considered when determining if presoaking is necessary. As much as possible you want to ensure that you do not harm yourself or open the door for others to harm you more than what may have already been experienced.

This process may take a while. It is ok to sit a little and soak.

Consider the following questions when determining if presoaking is necessary.

What are your issues or concerns?

____

____

____

____

____

How long have they been concerns?

____

____

____

____

____

Was the issue self-inflicted? Yes ☐ No ☐
If yes, how?

____

____

____

____

____

Are others involved? Yes ☐ No ☐
If so, what is their relationship to you?

____
____
____
____
____

Is your heart connected to those other people?
Yes ☐ No ☐

CHAPTER 3 REFLECTION
THINK ABOUT IT

What will be the cleaning agent(s) that you use? Will you seek support and balance from: a therapist, family, friends, support groups, mentors, church family, preachers, priests, physical activities, etc.

____

____

____

____

____

What steps will you take to access those cleaning agent(s) you have chosen?

____

____

____

____

____

Chapter 4
Hit Start

Your process is about to become intense.

Congratulations! Yes, I said congratulations. You are almost there, and this is something to be proud of. You should always celebrate your progress along the way. During this time, you will begin to discuss and address your issues. This can be done with a traditional therapist, spiritual leader, accountability partner, friend, family member, support person, or a quiet conversation with you and God. Understand that different issues and experiences may need more than one outlet to go through the situation and begin the cleansing and healing process.

Now that you have laid it all out, identified the issues, made the necessary preparation, thought it through, it is time to hit start. Please understand that this process will not be easy. During this process you may feel uncomfortable. There may be steps during this process that you do not agree with or moments when you think you cannot continue. As the water rises you may feel like you are drowning, the temperature of the water may be too hot or too cold, the cleaning agent may appear to be too strong, the back and forth motion may make you feel a little ill, the agitation is meant to and will do just that, agitate you, the aggressive spinning may have your mind and emotions in a place of uncertainty, but trust me it will all be worth it.

After you put in all the work and go through your process, you will feel much better.

WHAT DO YOU NEED TO HIT START?

This is the specific time that you look at exactly what you need. This is not an overall look at what should be done, or what will make others feel better. No, what do YOU need to hit start? The process began when you realized that you would need to do your laundry, but now you are about to actively start the process. There is a difference between knowing that something must change and actively taking part in the change. Are you ready?

WHAT IS YOUR MENTAL AND EMOTIONAL STATE?

Why is it important to evaluate your psychological state before embarking on a journey of healing? Have you ever heard the saying: *Be careful what you think because your thoughts become your words and your words become your actions and your actions become your habits?*

There is so much truth to this saying. Before words, actions or habits manifest there is a thought. Our mind is so powerful. Your mind (brain) is the epicenter of your thoughts and feelings. If you are not in a place of stable thoughts then your judgement may be off, and you may not begin this journey with the necessary foundation. Those scattered thoughts can lead to emotionally unstable decisions. This process can literally be a life or death situation you cannot afford to make unstable decisions.

There are times that we attempt to make very important decisions without evaluating our mental and emotional state. Personally, I know that I have been in a situation where I was going to make an important decision while mentally and emotionally unstable. Years ago, I was struggling with a decision to resign from my place of employment. There were a series of events that happened, and I realized it was no longer a healthy environment.

One afternoon I was driving through an unfamiliar neighborhood trying to find the address of a client. After almost an hour, I finally found the house. I knocked on the door. There was no answer, although I saw someone looking out the curtains. I continued to knock for a couple minutes, and then I decided to leave. I was fuming at this point! I decided the next day I would let my boss know that I quit! I had been submitting resumes for weeks but had not received any responses. My decision to abruptly resign would not have been the best decision because I did not have a plan. My decision was also emotionally driven.

As a single mother of twins, I knew I needed a job, but I was not thinking straight. As I began driving back to my office, I began to pray. Now I will be honest, mixed in with my prayer was an ultimatum to God. Imagine that. But we do it. I said, "God, If I don't find a job by the 15th of this month, I am quitting without a job." I continued praying and crying. I knew prayer would help settle my mind and emotions. My alone time with God brought a sense of calm over me, and I decided not to make an irrational decision.

Two days later I received a job offer. I am grateful that I chose to pray before I made a potentially unhealthy decision.

WHAT IS YOUR SPIRITUAL STATE?

Are you connected to a power "higher" than yourself? I understand that people have different views on who God is to them and how they are connected to their own God. While traveling on your personal journey to healing and cleansing the stains of your life, you will have to understand that you are not the ultimate being. There is indeed a power stronger and mightier than you. This is not to say that you must be connected to one specific religion or belief system. However, I firmly believe that on your journey it is a must that you have an understanding that you are not all powerful.

There will be times when you feel that you are being let down by people. It is important that you have a sense of spiritual connection. When people fail you, and they will, you can rely on something bigger than all of us.

WHAT IS THE STATE OF YOUR SELF-AWARENESS?

Are you aware of who you are, your motives, your character, your values? Who are you? Are you what others say about you? Do you identify and define yourself by the stains of your life? These are questions to consider when evaluating your own self-awareness. You want to be certain that during this process you are in touch with your authentic self. If by chance you think that your authentic self is too damaged and that you "are who you are," please rethink this. You are never too damaged, hurt, traumatized, or abused not to be healed. Those stains can be cleaned. Yes, you may have had experiences that have created character flaws, but this is not who you are at the core. This is a defeatist mindset. A defeatist mindset encourages you to constantly expect the worse. Try to be the person who can see the glass half full versus half empty. In doing this apply it to who you are and who you can be through the process of getting in touch with your true self.

I believe that good is in every person, unfortunately life experiences may impact behaviors. Often these behaviors are means of surviving or coping with your life stains. Take some time to get to truly know who you are. Choose to be easy on yourself and allow room to heal and grow.

WHAT ARE YOUR IDENTIFIED ISSUES BEING ADDRESSED?

Do you know what your "issues" are? I know you may know how situations, people or places may make you feel, but can you truly identify those things that have caused stains in your life? These stains have been the reason you have feelings of hurt but where does your hurt stem from? I am referring to the hurt that has led to brokenness. You are preparing to hit start on your cleansing processes. It is important to not only be aware of your mental, emotional, spiritual and self-awareness you must be clear about the stains and brokenness to move forward so that the process is fruitful and positive.

If you identify a laundry stain on the front of your shirt, you may think it looks like some sort of red juice, but you are not quite sure. We have all been there when we look down at our shirt and say, "Now how did I do that?" Most of the time it is something red. I am not sure why, but that is usually the color of the stain.

When preparing to wash your clothes it would be helpful if you are able to identify the origin of the stain. You would treat a red juice stain differently than a red wine stain. The reason is because red wine and red juice are treated differently, so you must be clear as to the stain that you are trying to rid your fabric of.

Although this example may seem trivial and not relative to situations of significant stains such as trauma or abuse, the point is you must be able to identify those issues that are going to be addressed. This will allow your piece of fabric to come out clean. Remember you are the fabric; you have delicate needs that must be approached with care and diligence. It should not be taken lightly.

I know that some of this may seem overwhelming. Your cleansing process will require you to dig deep. You may uncover some things that you thought were buried way below the surface of who you may have convinced yourself and others that you are. But it is time to hit start.

Disclaimer: All washing machines are not the same. However, they all have the same purpose.

Once you hit start your machine may begin shaking a bit because it is attempting to check for the size of the load. This is important for balance. Do not be afraid. Balance and stabilization are good. It helps to ensure the process will be effective. When you hit start to begin addressing the stains of your life, your body, mind, and spirit may begin to shake a bit because it too is trying to create a balance and protect your personal machine.

Next, as the water begins to fill up fear may set in and you may think to yourself that this is too much, and you think you need to stop. Just breathe it is all a part of the process. Remember the machine already performed the function of sensing the load that was put in, so the balance was already created. In addition, you have done a lot of work to prepare for this moment. You have already considered your mental, emotional, and spiritual state. You have explored the state of your self-awareness and identified the issues that need to be addressed. You owe it to yourself and the valuable fabrics in the washer to push through until the end. I know it is uncomfortable. Trust me, you can do it.

CHAPTER 4 REFLECTION
THINK ABOUT IT

Are you ready to hit the start button on your process?
Yes ☐ No ☐

If yes, how?

____

____

____

____

____

If not, what do you think is holding you back?

____

____

____

____

____

Take a moment to think about the questions posed in Chapter 4:

What is your mental and emotional state?

What is your spiritual state?

What is the state of your self-awareness?

What are your identified issues being addressed?

NOTES

Chapter 5
The Agitation

Bring It!

This is the section of the book I have been waiting for. This section is the entire reason that I decided to write this book. In 2003 while working at a Drug and Alcohol Halfway House for women as the Resource Coordinator, I encountered a young woman I will call Sally. Sally came into my office and she was visibly agitated. She told me that she received a letter to appear in court. She was upset because she had been in the program for about 3 months and was doing well. Sally could not understand why this was happening now. I casually told Sally that it is like your clothes being washed. They must go through the agitation stage to become clean. I told Sally that this was her agitation stage.

I explained to her that although she was clean and, in a program, she would still be responsible to address the "wreckage of her past." Although her wreckage was illegal activity that took place during her addiction, she would have to go through a process to become whole. Unfortunately, in most cases we do not have the luxury of leaving small fires as we travel through life and expect that it will not catch up to us at some point.

I often encounter people who have the mindset that if they are "doing good" now, they can disregard all that they may have done in their past that has negatively impacted others. Take this young woman for instance, while in her addiction, she committed crimes. She stole from others, sold and purchased illegal substances. She was arrested, charged and sent to jail. She was released on bail but did not show for court. After a while, she decided it was time to clean her life up, so she made the decision to enter treatment. To be clear, this was a great decision. It was not only great for her, but for her children, family and friends who were desperately waiting for the day that she took the leap into the world of recovery. None of this changed the fact that she committed crimes during her active addiction and these actions now would need to be addressed.

I completely understood her agitation. By sharing the analogy of washing clothes and the agitation stage of this process, I hoped that she would understand and relate it to her current life situation. Thankfully she did. Although she struggled with the decision to attend her court hearing, she did attend. Her initial thoughts were to leave the program just in case the authorities came to look for her. Through our conversation and a call to her family who essentially begged her not to run and to face her responsibility, she remained in the program. She attended her court hearing with a letter from our program, her sponsor and family. To her surprise the judge ordered for her to complete the program and scheduled a court date for after her program completion date. She was elated to say the least. In her mind she had conjured up every worst-case scenario possible and was certain she would not be able to remain in the program, sent back to jail, and be forced to start her process all over again. The agitation that she was feeling precluded her from thinking straight, which then caused her to almost make an emotionally driven decision.

Although this specific story may not speak directly to you because you may not be in recovery from substances, there are other situations in which our life choices must be addressed at a later point of our life. Most of the time when we are faced with potential consequences as a result of our own choices it does not happen at an opportune time. The consequences are not typically what we envision or desire. It would be great if we could schedule and determine what our potential agitation or consequences will be. I would schedule mine when life is great, relationships are healthy, I am stable in my mind, body and spirit, my finances are stable, my employment and business is stable, you know, not a care in the world. Yup, that is the best time, bring the consequences. Also, I would make sure they caused minimal disruption to my life. I do not think that would be asking too much. But that is not at all how life works.

As a person in leadership for the past 10 years at various employers with varying types of work, all within the helping profession, I have come to the realization that consequences never happen at an opportune time. For instance, I have witnessed situations in which a person was not adhering to agency policy and/or procedure. They were given warnings, coaching, unpaid time off, but the behaviors continued. They were advised the next step could lead to termination. Unfortunately, the behaviors continued, and the employee was ultimately terminated. Without fail, the person begins to express all the things that just happened in their life and they "cannot be terminated now!"

I think it is very rare that there is a perfect time to be terminated from a job, although I know many people have said, "I wish they would just fire me." I do not truly think that is the most professional way to exit. Like the young lady at the treatment facility, often these employees were allowing their agitation to guide their behaviors which ultimately led to an untimely consequence.

Parents often must bear witness to untimely consequences for their children. I believe our children often forget that we were young once. As a matter of fact, we were their age at one time. For some reason I think our children have this thought in their mind that we were born, and then became "old." That has always baffled me. I often find myself saying to my children, "I know because I was your age before. I made some decisions that resulted in untimely consequences and my desire for you is that you will not experience these same things." Much like other parents/caregivers our advice falls on deaf ears. We usually are reintroduced into the conversation once the agitation begins and they are forced to deal with the consequences of their behaviors. This is not a comfortable feeling, but it is the reality. My suggestion is to continue to support your children by helping guide them to an understanding of the agitation stages in their life. Hopefully, they will come to understand agitation is necessary to cleanse themselves of those things that may be weighing them down.

I am often encouraged when I encounter others, or I make a choice myself to embrace the agitation. It is through the agitation process that we can learn and grow. I truly believe agitation helps us to develop into better people. It can be looked at as our crossroads, will we go right or left. It is decision time.

Embrace the agitation!

What happens during the agitation stage during the washing process? During the agitation stage, the articles of clothing are stirred up, they are moved around through the water and detergent. The process is intended to create such a disturbance with the clothing that the dirt is forced to be removed from the clothing. This is needed for your clothing to be cleansed. It is a good thing. What would happen if the agitation process was removed from the wash cycles? The clothes, detergent, and water would sit in the washer. Then the rinse cycle would start, then finish with the spin cycle. It is very unlikely that those clothes with the stains and possible stench would become clean. Those items of clothing may be rid of the surface dirt, but the stains and stench will remain. Why? Because for the interwoven parts of the fabric to be impacted, that agitation will need to occur. The clothes will need to be moved around.

Like the process of cleaning your own life stains and stench, to address these things, it is a must that you go beneath the surface. You must be made uncomfortable, shaken up a bit. When you add your cleaning agent to the process regardless if you choose: a therapist, family, friends, support groups, mentors, church family, preachers, priests, physical activities, etc., it will be imperative that you go beyond the surface. I know it may be difficult because the agitation brings the uncomfortable issues to the surface. This is necessary so that those things can eventually be washed away.

Years ago, I decided to begin counseling sessions with a therapist. Reflecting on that experience I now realize why it was not as effective as it could have been. I attempted to control the experience from start to finish. Once I was assigned a clinician, I attended my first session. Well, I thought she "jumped" into my personal business too fast." To this day I laugh at that, it was less about how she chose to engage me and more about my state of mind and emotions at the time. I was trying to control my experience by requesting a different clinician and surprisingly enough I was given one without an objection. At the beginning of my next session I made sure to tell the new clinician all the reasons why I thought it did not work with her colleague.

I did not understand that the first experience was my agitation, and I needed it. Although I did not agree with the approach the point was to help me grow and address my issues. I was uncomfortable and decided to flee. Although I worked through my life stains that were prevalent at that time, it is possible the process of healing may not have taken as long if I had embraced the agitation.

THE UNCOMFORTABLE FEELING OF BEING AGITATED

Who seeks out agitation in their life? I have not met anyone that deliberately seeks out agitation. Although, deliberate actions may result in being agitated through possible consequences, I do not believe people wake up and say, "Let me get agitated today." Seeking out agitation and embracing agitation is two different things.

Seeking out agitation can be viewed as an unhealthy way of coping with what may be a deeper issue. It may be a way of deflecting what you may be upset about. For example, you and your significant other had a disagreement in the morning before you left for work. There was a whole book of thoughts that you wished you had said, but you did not. You held onto those words, but you were still agitated. Once you arrive at work you were still upset. You begin to calm down about an hour into your workday, but the agitated feeling is still resonating with you. It is now lunch time. You go to the staff kitchen and put your food in the microwave, walk to the restroom while it is heating up. When you return you notice your bowl is on the counter and someone else is standing in front of the microwave with their food now heating up. They turn to you and graciously say hello and begin to let you know they took the liberty of taking your food out because it started boiling over. They even cleaned up the spill. Unfortunately, you cannot hear them because your blood is now boiling over. You let loose with a barrage of insults about how inconsiderate they are for not waiting for you. You completely disregard why they removed your food or that they cleaned up your mess. You decided to act on your agitation regarding a situation that did not deserve the behavior that you were displaying. You were already agitated about a much bigger situation that happened at home and sought out a way to finish the conversation from earlier in the morning.

There are times that we project or misread a situation, and we create unnecessary agitation for ourselves. It takes time, but it is advantageous to learn how to embrace agitation instead of seeking it out to deflect what you may truly be dealing with.

Embracing agitation is a healthy way of coping and moving forward from issues that have caused your agitation. When you embrace something with the expectation that the result will help you to grow and learn from the experience you will handle the agitation differently. This is not to say that you may not be annoyed by the agitation, but the way you think about and respond to it will be different.

There was a time that I folded under the pressure of agitation. Yes, I folded, I did not break, but the pressure of the agitation can be difficult to handle. Now that I am older, and I have experienced varying degrees of agitation, I look at it differently. I understand that agitation is a necessary part of the process and there are challenges in life that are meant to cause agitation.

In chapter 4, I said: *Be careful what you think because your thoughts become your words and your words become your actions and your actions become your habits.* Choosing to have a positive thought about situations that appear to be disruptions in your life will greatly impact how you handle them. We are all human and not one of us is perfect so there are times we will fall short. But I encourage you to adopt the mindset that everything happens for a reason and there is a lesson to be learned from every situation. You may not know what the lesson is at that moment, but trust that the agitation will contribute to your growth and life lessons learned.

CHAPTER 5 REFLECTION
THINK ABOUT IT

What are points of agitation in your life?

What will you actively do to embrace your agitation?

How will you change your thinking?

How will you change your behaviors?

Chapter 6
Rinse Cycle

Am I drowning?

The entire process of washing clothes can be a bit exhausting. Depending on how many loads you may have and the depth of the laundry stains, you may feel like you will never complete the task. Although it may be overwhelming it is necessary. You cannot afford to allow the dirt and stains to go unaddressed and the stench to take over your life.

The rinse cycle is just as important as all the other cycles of the process. During the rinse cycle the cleaning agent and dirt are rinsed out of the clothes. The clothes are tossed around in various directions to ensure that the process is complete. It is extremely important that the dirt is washed away.

As the water begins to saturate your fabric, it will be uncomfortable, and you may even feel like you are drowning. But you are not, you can handle this! Remember this is a part of the process, and if this does not happen, then the dirt will remain. When you started the process of cleaning YOUR laundry you recognized that there were issues in your life that would need to be addressed to help you become the best version of yourself that you could possibly be. There are significant benefits to sticking with the rinse process. Allowing the water to interact with your cleaning agent and rid your fabric of harmful stains can increase the positivity in your life and preserve your personal fabric. You may rid yourself of those unhealthy things that can be contributing to the breakdown of who you are. The peace that you can potentially gain from this process is priceless. So embrace the flow of the water.

Have you ever had a stressful day and all you wanted to do was go home, shower and rest? I have encountered many helping professionals who have expressed feeling this way. Helping professionals are people who nurture the growth of or address the problems of a person's physical, psychological, intellectual, emotional or spiritual well-being. Sometimes helping professionals feel like they are carrying the weight of the world on their shoulders. You interact with people all day and, in many cases, absorb their issues and concerns. Because of the intimate nature of the relationship, their life stains can become your stains. It can be very overwhelming and by the end of the day you just need to rid yourself of these stains. It is not healthy to carry others weight (stressors), you have your own that you need to be cleansed from.

Once you get home, set your things down, retreat to the bathroom, and turn on the shower to the temperature that best suits you. Hot is my desired temperature. Once you step into the shower, it is like you can literally feel the stress and issues of the day washing off your body. You add the cleaning agent and allow the water and your cleaning agent to begin working. This is a good feeling. Just stand there for a moment and allow the water to run over your body, allow the process of washing away the weight of the day. Take a deep breath and exhale. You can literally see the mixture of the water and cleaning agent slowly disappear down the drain. It is as if all the issues from others is washed away. This is what it feels like when you do your laundry. It leads to a feeling of relaxation and cleanliness.

WHAT ABOUT YOU?

The previous example was of rinsing away the stains of others, but what about you? It is very easy for us to identify the life stains of others. We often find ourselves in conversations discussing others, their short comings or issues. But what about you? We can sit and have an entire conversation about who is on drugs, committed or committing crimes, cheating, being cheated on, has been fired from their job, about to lose their home, car was repossessed, lost their children, so forth and so on. But what about you?

When your fabrics are in the rinse cycle the water is literally pouring over the clothing and detergent to wash away the dirt and stains that were brought to the surface from deep in the fabric. These may have been stains that would potentially cause more damage than we thought. Things that lay beneath the surface are often invisible with a quick glance. It is not until you begin moving things around that you realize, there was more to the problem than you thought.

ARE YOU READY FOR YOUR DOWNPOUR?

I think you are. At this point, you have truly invested time, energy, humbled yourself and allowed yourself to become vulnerable to the process. You have exhibited courage and strength. It takes both to admit you have an issue that should be addressed. Regardless if this issue is by way of your personal choices or due to someone else's actions you recognize that in order to be a better you, these issues need to be addressed. Allow the cleaning agent of your choice to work with the water, move around and embrace the uncomfortable feelings so all areas can be fully cleansed.

Chapter 7
The Spin Cycle
You May Feel Nauseous

There is a medical condition called Vertigo and many people suffer from it. It is an inner ear disorder that causes, dizziness, nausea, ringing of the ear and difficulty balancing. This feeling often happens after your brain has been signaled that your surroundings are spinning. I am getting nauseous just thinking about the times that I have had this feeling. It is an uncomfortable feeling. Vertigo increases with age. This is probably why, as children, being dizzy was fun. Most adults do not seek out experiences that they know will cause Vertigo. But surprisingly, as kids, those were the games and toys that we found most exciting. Think back to the games and toys that you played with as a child: the merry go round, tire swing, duck, duck goose, baseball spin, running around in circles for no real reason, just because you were young and making up things to do. My all-time favorite spinning game was THE SIT AND SPIN! As an only child for the first 10 years of my life, I often thought of games to do alone. The Sit and Spin was my favorite but had no real purpose. There was no winner or loser, you did not collect money or prizes. You would just sit and spin. Yup, that was fun as a child, and we did not need a purpose.

Then comes adulthood, and, unfortunately, that thing called purpose becomes important. Adult spinning is different. It can cause dizziness, be very uncomfortable, and not "fun", but it is necessary. During the spin cycle, the washer drains, and the machine spins rapidly. This is a pace that we cannot control. You may feel a little tight as the spin cycle increases. That is ok, at least you know that the stains and stench were removed.

You must allow the machine to operate the way that it is intended. That may be difficult for you, but you are going through a life changing process and this is not the time to be the director, but time to take direction. This is difficult for some of us. The mere thought that you will participate in a process that you cannot control and do not know the outcome of may make you feel uncomfortable. Remember that this process was never meant to make you feel comfortable, but just the opposite, the process was to make you so uncomfortable that you are driven to make a change.

During this cycle you may feel like your emotions and thoughts are going round and round. You may feel like you are not grounded. Your head is literally spinning with all the what ifs. But you are now beyond the what ifs. You are here now and working on finalizing your cleansing process and it will be worth it.

The machine stops. Initially it is as if all your issues are sticking together. The fabric begins to regain control as the spinning comes to an end. Those articles of clothing that appeared stuck together are now falling from the side of the washing machine barrel and beginning to slightly separate. You smell the freshness; you see the brightness of the fabric that was once covered with stains. You can breathe a sigh of relief because your laundry is now clean. Despite the feeling of nausea and being out of control you survived.

"Despite the feeling of nausea and being out of control you survived.`

PART III
Finishing Touches

"I survived because the fire inside me burned brighter than the fire around me."

~Joshua Graham

Although you have completed the process of washing your clothes, you are not quite done yet. You must dry, fold and put them away.

Depending on the instructions on the fabric's label the temperature of the drying process can reach about 135 degrees Fahrenheit. Now that is hot.

The purpose of drying your clothes is to put the finishing touches on the process. This also may help you to avoid the pain of unnecessarily starting your cleansing process all over again. Although the spin cycle removes most of the excess water from your clothes, they are still wet. More than likely you will not choose to wear wet clothes fresh out of the washing machine. Therefore, it will be important to dry them. You can either air dry them or put them in the dryer.

When you remove your clothes from the washer be mindful of the instructions on the label. For instance:

LINE DRY

Hang the item or garment from a line or bar, indoors or out. Tumbling dry could damage this item.

TUMBLE DRY, NORMAL

You can dry the item in a machine at up to the hottest setting. A system of dots indicates the recommended temperature range, from low to high.

DOTS

The more dots you see on the tag mean the more heat the clothes can take. One dot means cool or low heat, two dots for warm or medium heat, and three dots for hot or high temperature.

DASHES

As for dashes, the more dashes you see, the gentler of a cycle you should use. One dash means permanent press cycle, two dashes means gentle/delicate cycle, and dash in the shape of an "X" mean do not wash.

You have done a lot of work thus far and you want to make sure your process was not in vain.

If you choose not to dry your clothes and allow them to sit while wet, they may develop a mildew smell and you are right back where you started, with a stench. I do not care how much "smell good" you apply to mildew it will still have a stench. When you encounter others, they will smell you immediately. The stench of your past ills, and unhealthy characteristics that you worked so hard to overcome during your cleansing process will have to be addressed again, but from the beginning of the process. Do not create more work for yourself or make this process harder than it must be.

Folding, Hanging and Putting Away

The next thing you will have to do to complete the process is fold and/or hang and put your clothing away. Personally, I have grown to appreciate washing and even drying but the final steps often seems pointless. I mean after all I am going to wear the clothing again so just pull them from the hamper or the pile at the foot of my bed, right? Wrong!

This step not only creates order in your surroundings, but this too can prevent you from having to start your process over again. For example, have you ever washed and dried a load of laundry, but not fold/hang and put them away? You either leave them in the hamper or in a pile somewhere else in your home. A week or two go by and you reach into that pile to grab something. Low and behold you cannot remember if you washed it or not. So, what do you do? You usually smell it first and hold it up to the light to check for obvious stains. Ok, well maybe that is just me. Then you say, well I will just wash it again, just in case. When you very well may have already washed it. But because you allowed it to sit and not put it away you cannot tell if it was mixed in with the loads that you have yet to clean.

Think about the loads that you have already completed. In some cases, you have exhausted yourself identifying, separating, and cleansing your loads. Do you really want to start over from the beginning because you did not complete the process?

I have been in a situation where I was working on managing the personal loads that I have, and because I did not complete the process, I had to start over. I could not remember what I addressed and where I was making progress. When you interrupt your process, you face the danger of having to start the process over.

Appreciate your process enough not to create more work for yourself.

Final Thoughts

You should be proud of yourself. This process is not easy. As a matter of fact, it can be quite tedious. The acknowledgment and acceptance that you have dirty laundry can be difficult for people. It is hard to admit that you may have some undesirable personal attributes in your life. It is even more difficult when you realize you have been carrying them for a long time and they are beginning to negatively impact you and possibly your relationships. The amazing news is that you made the choice to invest in yourself and take the necessary steps to become a healthier you.

> "The chaos of the dirty laundry pile will be eliminated."

Although stains may reemerge you will be better equipped to address them. You were successful at going through each cycle in your process and being intentional as to what you learned along the way.

You will no longer allow those negative traits or life experiences to control your life. The chaos of the dirty laundry pile will be eliminated. You now understand the importance of addressing issues as they arise so that they will no longer cause you harm.

Be well and continue to love you,
Maisha

W.A.S.H.

(Withstand all Strife to Heal)

About the Author

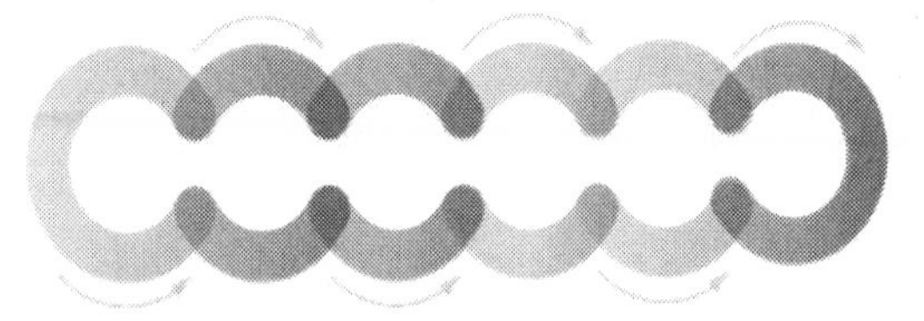

At a young age, Maisha Howze was groomed to be aware of, and empathetic to the plight of her community and those closely related. Coming from a big family rich in community service and activism, Ms. Howze's upbringing exposed her to positive building of her marginalized community. This awareness raised a sincere dedication and commitment to the field of social services. Maisha has worked in the social services field for more than 20 years and is currently the Administrator for the Allegheny County Department of Human Services, Office of Behavioral Health, Bureau of Drug and Alcohol Services (BDAS). BDAS is responsible for the planning, implementation, evaluation and technical assistance of contracted drug and alcohol providers in Allegheny County. Through this position, she strives to provide quality care to individuals and families in Allegheny County.

Ms. Howze is passionate about volunteering. As a member of Macedonia Church of Pittsburgh, she supports her community through various church initiatives. She also volunteers in several other capacities including: 412 Food Rescue as a Food Rescue Hero, Pennsylvania Organization for Women in Early Recovery (POWER) for special events, and as a mentor to young women with similar life experiences.

InTouch
consulting

References

Lauren Hill. "Laundry Basics: How to Choose the Washing Cycle" (October 26, 2010) www.mamaslaundrytalk.com

Home and Garden. www.homeandgarden.com

Taylor Flannery. Household Management 101 www.householdmanagement101.com

How Stuff Works. www.howstuffworks.com

NOTES

NOTES

NOTES

Made in the USA
Columbia, SC
06 December 2020